POCAHONTAS

Library of Congress Number: 84-9819

Library of Congress Cataloging in Publication Data

Gleiter, Jan, 1947-
 Pocahontas.

 Summary: A biography of the Powhatan Indian woman who
befriended the English settlers at Jamestown, Virginia, and
helped maintain peace between her tribe and the colonists.
 1. Pocahontas, d. 1617—Juvenile literature.
2. Powhatan Indians—Biography—Juvenile literature.
3. Smith, John, 1580-1631—Juvenile literature.
4. Jamestown (Va.)—History—Juvenile literature.
5. Virginia—History—Colonial period, ca. 1600-1775—
Juvenile literature. [1. Pocahontas, d. 1617. 2. Powhatan
Indians. 3. Indians of North America—Virginia. 4. Smith,
John, 1580-1631. 5. Jamestown (Va.)—History. 6. Virginia
—History—Colonial period, ca 1600-1775] I. Thompson,
Kathleen. II. Chabrian, Deborah, ill. III. Title.
E99.P85P5734 1984   975.5'01'0924 [B] [92] 84-9819
ISBN 0-8172-2118-2 lib. bdg.
ISBN 0-8172-2261-8 softcover

POCAHONTAS

Jan Gleiter and Kathleen Thompson
Illustrated by Deborah L. Chabrian

Raintree Childrens Books
Milwaukee · Toronto · Melbourne · London

4

Many years ago in England, a woman named Lady Rebecca Rolfe was walking through a garden. She was thinking about a young Indian girl named Pocahontas. Lady Rebecca sat down on a bench and closed her eyes. Her memory took her back to America, back to Virginia and a small, Indian village. She could remember many things.

One morning, angry shouts had awakened the ten-year-old Indian girl. Pocahontas lay quietly, listening to the voices of her father and the other Indian men.

"They are here again! White men!"

The angry voices went on, talking about the other white men who had come before. The Indians had not forgotten them. They had been bad men, cruel men, who had lied to the Indians and had killed their people. Now there were more of these white men. They were camped not too far away, near the great water.

Pocahontas slipped from her bed. She was curious. She ran, barefoot, through the forest. She wanted to see these coat-wearing people, just once.

Pocahontas could hear shouts in the distance. She moved closer. Through the trees, she saw four boys turning cartwheels. It looked like fun. Pocahontas loved any kind of game. In fact, *Pocahontas* was a nickname given to her by her father. It meant "playful one."

Pocahontas ran into the clearing. She turned three cartwheels in a row and landed on her feet in front of the surprised boys. That was the beginning of a new friendship for her, a friendship with white settlers.

As the weeks went by, Pocahontas often visited Jamestown. That was the name of the English settlers' village. She played leapfrog and other games with the four boys. She made friends with some of the older people. One of them became a special friend. His name was John Smith.

John Smith was curious about the Indians, just as Pocahontas was curious about the settlers. He wanted to learn the Indians' language. Pocahontas wanted to learn the settlers' language. They spent hours teaching each other.

"Tomahawk," said Pocahontas, pointing to John Smith's ax.

"Kettle," said John Smith, pointing to a copper pot cooking over the fire.

Before long, each of them could talk a little in the other one's language.

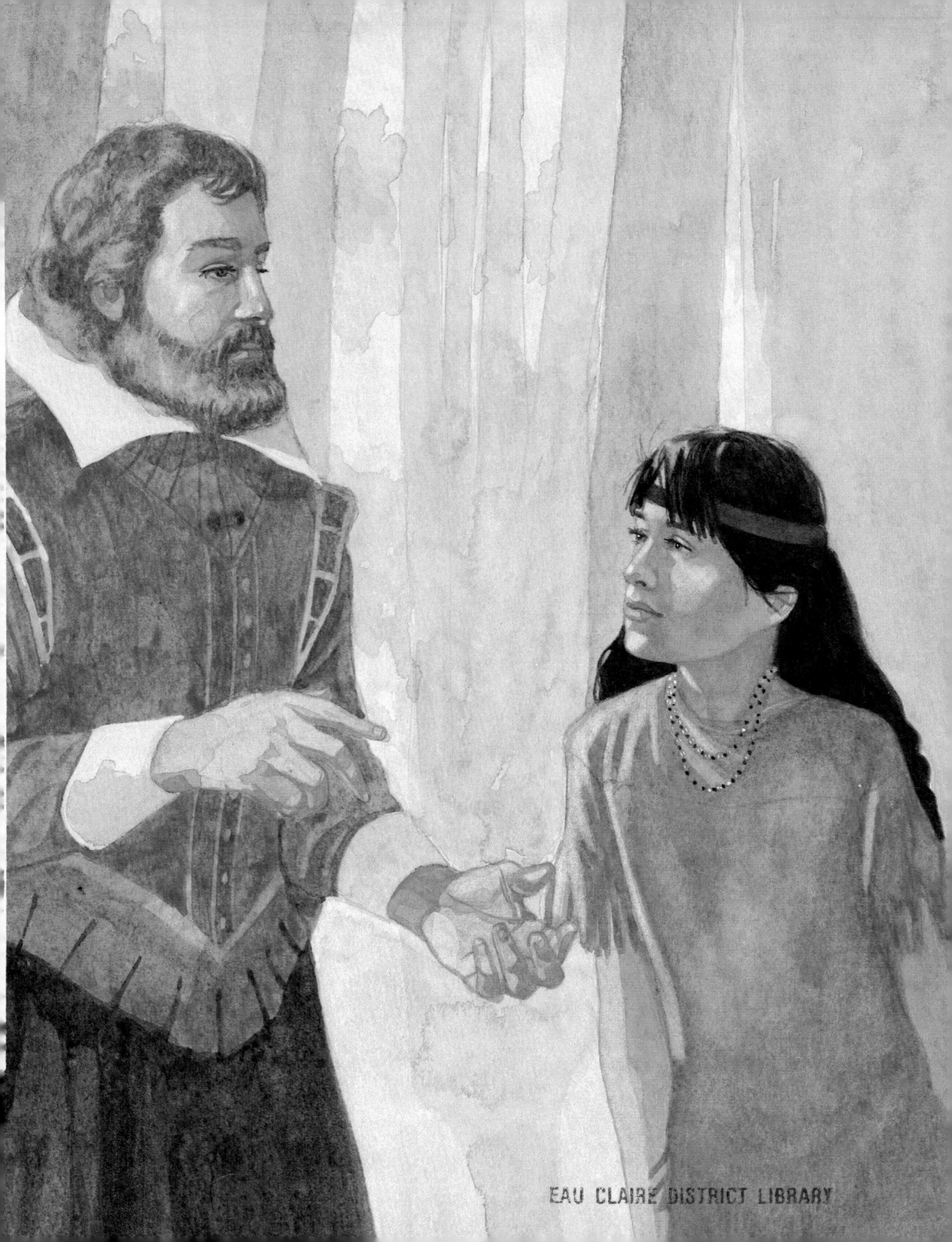

Pocahontas's father was the leader of the Indians in that part of Virginia. His name was Powhatan. He did not feel as Pocahontas did. He did not like the settlers, and he did not want them on the Indians' land.

Some of the settlers were killed by Indian arrows. Soon settlers stopped going into the woods to hunt because of the danger. Their food supply was running out, and they had no way to get more. They called it "The Starving Time."

P ocahontas worried about her friends at Jamestown. Often, she took baskets of corn to them. She begged her brother to help. He and a few others took fish and small animals that they had killed in the forest. The settlers were grateful. Their small friend had saved many lives.

One winter afternoon, Pocahontas heard about a great feast in the Indian village. It was going to be held that night. Everyone was excited.

A white settler had been caught in the forest. Tonight he would be at the feast. Pocahontas's father would have to decide what to do with him.

Pocahontas went to the feast. She was near the back of the room, so she could not see who the settler was. Was he one of the men who had been friendly to her? She was afraid for him.

Everyone was in a good mood. There was a lot of laughter. After dinner, two large stones were dragged to the center of the room. The settler was pulled to the stones. Then he was pushed down on the ground, and his head was placed on one of the stones. Several Indians jumped forward. They carried clubs.

Suddenly, Pocahontas knew what would happen. The Indians were going to smash the settler's head with the clubs and kill him.

Pocahontas moved to the front of the crowd. She saw that the man with his head on the stone was John Smith.

Pocahontas's heart jumped with fright. But she did not cry or scream. Crying and screaming would not help her friend. Instead, she ran forward. As the Indians raised their clubs, she fell to the ground beside John Smith. Softly, she placed her head against his. Now if the clubs came down, they would crush her. If her father wanted to kill her friend, he would have to kill his favorite daughter, too.

Powhatan let out a shout. "Stop!"

For several moments, Powhatan thought. Pocahontas remained still. She dared not even whisper in the ear so close to her lips. She would not beg for her life. The minutes dragged by.

Powhatan made up his mind. "Free him!" he ordered.

John Smith was free to go back to his own people. For a while there was peace between the Indians and the settlers. But then the fighting began again.

S ome of the settlers had a plan. They decided to
kidnap Pocahontas. They hoped that it would
make Powhatan agree to stop fighting. After all,
Pocahontas was his dearest child.

   The settlers caught Pocahontas and took her back
to live with them. They taught her how to live as
they lived. They changed her name.

   Powhatan was not worried about his child. He
knew that the settlers would treat her well.

A man named John Rolfe fell in love with the beautiful Indian girl. He asked her to marry him, and Pocahontas agreed. Later, they had a son. And still later, John Rolfe asked Pocahontas to go on a long trip with him, to England.

The trip was dangerous. But Pocahontas said that she would go. She hoped that it would help the English to understand her people. Also, it might make them more willing to help the settlers in America. She was right.

Now Pocahontas was in England. She was tired. She had been sick for much of her visit. But the trip was a big success, and Pocahontas became famous. Everyone called her by her new name, Lady Rebecca Rolfe.

S he sighed softly. She wished that she were at
home again, where the trees did not grow in
such neat rows as they did in the English gardens.
But she would stay as long as she was needed to help
people to learn to understand each other.

Her name had changed. Her life had changed. But
her good, brave heart had not.